Take Me Away

Flairs and Glairs

Publication House

"Take Me Away"

ISBN No: " 978-93-91302-51-1"
1ˢᵗ Edition
Language – English and Hindi

Flairs and Glairs
Publication House
Regd. Under MSME Act.

Disclaimer

This is a work of fiction and solely represent the thoughts of the corresponding authors of the articles. Our editors have tried their best to edit the content of all the authors and check the plagiarism.

All the write-ups in this book are unique and are only published in this book.

In case any plagiarism or error is found, only the author is responsible alone, and not the publisher or the Compilers.

Cover Designing and Book Formatting
Shubham Shah and Ishani Agarwal

Acknowledgement

My primary thanks to God. I am blessed with the energy to be able to complete this anthology.
I also thankful towards our whole team of "Flairs and Glairs Publication".

I am thankful to my parents for trusting and supporting me always. And my friends and extended family to support in every step of life. And to provide me a surrounding where I can raise my voice for all types of issues.

Thank you all the co-authors, without your support we would never be able to complete this anthology.

Co-Authors

Shubham Shah (Founder of Flairs and Glairs)
Ishani Agrawal (Co-founder Flairs and Glairs)
Muskan Shah (Project Head)
Jennifer Lazarus (Compiler)

1. Adam Voytecek
2. Chiara Stigum
3. Faisal
4. Rijul Alfred
5. Jenisha Shah
6. Cindella Brown
7. Lindiwe Sakala
8. Manqoba Mthethwa
9. Richard Charles Gwyn
10. Sohita Sapkotta
11. Nisha Saini
12. Tejasvi Manot
13. Sonia-Rose Lyle
14. Collins Takudzwa Birimhiri
15. Viziichu Kajiri
16. J Geer
17. Geeta Shukla
18. Sri Lasya Jillella
19. Sandy Salt
20. Ariel

Shubham Shah

(Founder- Flairs and Glairs)

Shubham Shah, an entrepreneur at "Flairs & Glairs" a brand with dynamics in events organizing and cultural educational pan INDIA, is a 26yrs old guy who recently has entered the digital platform of imprinting emotions. He has initiated with his own open mic platform to help budding poets and aspiring writers under his brand named as "Teekhe Zasbaaat"

He is a commerce graduate from the Bhagalpur City of Bihar.

He states Writing has impersonated him since childhood and he has now been writing for over a decade!

Cooking, on the other hand, is his passion! He also mentions, trying out new things just tickles him!

When asked sir, Why SPICY EMOTIONS?

He smiled and added, "agar jasbaat teekhe na ho toh wo jasbaat kahan" Spices are all that blends! So do his words!

As a chef, he presents to you his dish! Hot and freshly served! Taste it! Feel it! Enjoy it! You can also find his writing in the Book "Teekhe Zasbaaat" and 50+ Co-authored anthologies. With his passion to explore opportunities across Platforms, he is working with keen devotion and We wish him all the very best for his future ventures.

He is Featured in the International Magazine DeMode for his upcoming solo novel.

He is Approved by Ne8x for its Lit Fest, and is a Golden Star Awards 2020 Winner.

He is a India Book of Records Holder for his Anthology Satrang, and has the Grandmaster title by Asia Book of Records, for the same.

He has also been featured in Prabhat Khabar, Dainik Jagran, and a lot of other Newspapers in Bihar for his achievements.

He has been a proud co-author to

India Book Of Records (Title- Black)

World Book Of Records (Title -15 Wonders of Poetries)

India Book Of Records (Title - Aaina)

Vajra World Records Holder (Title - Gustakhi Maaf Hai)

High Range of Records Holder (Title - Gustakhi Maaf Hai)

Indian Book of Records

(Title - Road from Worst to Best)

Share your reviews on his

INSTAGRAM
@spicy_emotions
@shubham4shah
Or via email on
shubham2shah@gmail.com

To stay tuned to his work and opportunities follow his business Handles

INSTAGRAM   FACEBOOK   YOUTUBE

@flairsandglairs
@teekhezasbaaat

WEBSITE:
https://flairsandglairs.in/
https://flairsandglairs.com/

Ishani Agarwal

(Co-Founder- Flairs and Glairs)

Ishani Agarwal hails from the City of Joy, Kolkata.
She is the co-founder of her Community "Teekhe Zasbaaat" and Flairs and Glairs Publication.
Been a Compiler for 45+ Anthologies, she is in the process for more. Co-authored in 150+ Anthologies. She is a India Book of Records Holder, a Vajra World Records Holder, a High Range of Records Holder, an OMG Book of Records Holder, a Bravo Record holder, a Forever Star Book of World Records and an Indian Book of Records Holder.
Approved by Ne8x for its Lit Fest 2020, and Literary Icon 2020. Also a Golden Star Awards Winner 2020.
She has also been awarded with India Star Republic Award 2021, a part of She Awards by Awards Arc and Winner of Nari Samman 2021 by Literoma.

She is also selected as Best Achiever of the Year by AwardsArc and Most Challenging Compiler Award by Spectrum Awards.
She got her first solo Published,a solo Compilation consisting of first 750 contents of hers, titled "Hand That Burnt While Healing".

She has been featured by the National Magazine "Taree Zameen Par" with the title 'unstoppable'.
Also featured in the International Magazine DeMode for her upcoming solo novel, she is proud to write on social issues, and is happy with the love she is receiving.
Connect with her on Instagram: @Ishani_agarwal_quotes / @compilations_so_far

MUSKAN SHAH
PROJECT HEAD

'I follow dreams to make them reality'
Muskan Shah, a girl from Jharsuguda, Odisha. Currently a Company Secretary Professional Student, and an Interior Designer.

A writer and a Poetess.
Being a writer she writes all genre : stories, articles, quotes, content's, etc. And being a poetess she writes poetries and they are her forte.
Her journey till date has been amazing by being a compiler of 10 Anthologies and a co-author of 50+ Anthologies.

JENNIFER LAZARUS
<u>COMPILER</u>

Jennifer Lazarus is a writer, runner , keyboard player and a student from Mumbai. She's 19, young ambitious poet, also pursuing the management studies. Aspired in writings, as she feels it's the only way to express her feelings. She is a published co-author and a compiler who loves to fill her room with medals and trophies. In 2019, she was awarded for the best slogan writing. Her aim is to make other's happy with her poetry and musics

EMAIL- jennykad09@gmail.com

INSTAGRAM- @poem_pickk and @_jenniizzz

A Hint At What Is Beautiful

Beautiful is the "thank you"
When gracefully said,
Wrapped with humility,
What more can you spread?

Beautiful is your smile,
When that lip gives a curve,
To that every person you meet,
Isn't that heal, they deserve?

Beautiful is your heart,
With no regrets or hate,
Give them the part of it,
To who needs that beautiful shade.

Beautiful is your love,
Which you offer to all,
This is enough to break,
The rival's hatred wall.

Such thing matters in life,
Even if it's the smallest of small,
Know that your beautiful kind gesture,
Can help at somebody's fall.

Silence

There's a time at night,
When the world gets mute,
There's a complete silence,
But my mind plays flute.

I find myself,
In complete dark,
Silence has a sound,
For the memories, to unlock.

Now it's high time,
For such walls to break,
When my silence whispered,
"Wake up for the new memories to make"

ADAM VOYTECEK

Adam Voytecek is 35 years old and lives in Denver Colorado. He's been in love with writing for most of his life. Adam comes from a long back ground of writing song lyrics and recording music. He's very compassionate and loves nothing more in this world than his family and friends. His passions include reading, writing, music, horror, film, boxing, basketball and art. He has a 3 week old daughter, and she is his heart.

A Walk At Dusk

All is quiet on the suburban street as the lights come on. Only my footsteps and breath to disturb the silence. The sky looks like a painting from the mind of Bob Ross. A fox darts down the road and into a back yard. We both thought we were alone. This moment will forever remain a secret between us.
I walk down many streets with pleasant names as the sun fades. I pass many homes. Each with its own story. I imagine they are all good stories even though I'm sure some aren't. Heart ache and pain also dwell in many places. Something I know a lot about lately. Which is why I haven't gone back to my own home just yet. I think I'll take the long way and stay in my own world of happy homes just a little longer. Truth isn't going anywhere. And reality will be there when I'm ready to go back. In fact that's all that's waiting for me at home now. No need to rush.

Captives

If I took you on a tour
through my minds corridors
you should avoid the closet doors
Or say hello to the skeletons.
Some of them scream in there
It's like it's always Halloween in there
And though I'm ashamed of them
I can't blame them because I made them
only to lock the door and enslave them
And they may look scary
but the true monster is me
and they will try to expose that
so they can never be free

Salvation

February the 25th in 86
My destiny was paved
I was lost in the maze till I found salvation
in an instrumental tape
At the tender age my heart race
I get the chills when I think about the breaks
God showed me the light
Through Hip Hop I've been saved
It's my pills, my vice, my bottle, my razor blade
Take the pain away
So every time you see me write a rhyme
just know I'm giving praise

My Gifts

I have clinical depression
Plus I'm medicated for anxiety
Add some ADD in there
But don't feel bad for me
I'm ok with all that
We all have to live life
Those are the little imperfections
that make me me
Without those I probably couldn't
make the pen set fire to the paper
the way I can

Play

I push play and it reminds me
that I'm still alive
Have you ever smiled wide
and cried at the same time?
I've been drug free and still peaked
When those notes hit I get weak
Brought to my knees from the keys
Have you touched your spirit side
without going to church?
Have you found Heaven on earth?
I can time travel with no machine
Can you be awake and live a dream?
I can fly with no super powers
I can rise from the depths like a lotus flower
My aura can shine like the sun on the tide
I just close my eyes
Press play on that song
and know how it feels to be alive

CHIARA STIGUM

Chiara Stigum is a young woman who is enlisted in the US Air Force as a mechanic. While leading a very busy life she enjoys writing poetry in her free time; as well as, reading and spending time at the beach.

Red

When I gave you my
Vulnerability
I did not expect you to take my
Control
But you did it anyway
Rendering me defenseless
Giving me anxiety
Filling me with rage
So profound
It blurs my vision red

Seasonal Depression

The sun was out today
 I felt a little lighter, a little brighter
Like maybe the weight of the world
Was lifting off my shoulders and
I was finally starting to see in color

The day has come to end
I can only hope the sun
Will be out tomorrow again
Disappointed when I wake
To a world of gray and rain
Where the weight of the world
Is heavier than it's ever been

Dreams

As I lie awake
Staring up at the ceiling
I wonder what cruelty awaits
In my dreams
When I finally
Drift off to sleep

Warrioress

Her eyes gleam like the sun
And if you stare into them
You might even see her soul

She has a smile that can
Light up any room she walks into
And a laugh that resonates like music

You'd never guess the despair
Life has bestowed upon her
She's greatful for it all

Achievements

Nothing good in life is ever easy
Don't let the melancholy
Of the obstacles you face
Stop you from achieving your goals

FAISAL

Faisal hails from Johor Bahru, Johor, the southernmost city of Malaysia. He was born on 19 August 2002. He is the youngest in his family of seven. He is a Pokémon fan as it was his childhood companion. He loves, well, reading and writing, obviously.

Wind Therapy

Wind whispered in her ears
And washed her weary face
Blowing her blonde hair into waves
Of loose long black threads
Combing the elegant hair
Even though some had turned gray
Trying to take her along
But it would have to wait for a storm
But it did manage to take away
Some of her pains from yesterday
As it whispered in her ears
Telling "hey, it is okay"

Not Ugly

It is the angle. It is the mirror
It is the people, the camera and the picture
It is the dress. It is the hairstyle
It is the stress. It is the smile
It is the heart and cultural belief
There is a part you fail to notice
It is your thought and media influence
You are unique, not odd
There is a huge difference
Your kingdom of thought, only you can rule
No matter what, you are beautiful
You only are not to a blind fool
But you are to God if you are grateful
You are not ugly, yes, it is true
You are a beauty yet you do not have a clue
You have value. You are worthy
You just have to...see differently

Hey Listen

Forget all their words
Forgive their ignorance
You are not that easily offended
You cannot be hurt
You are not a mess
Stop comparing yourself
With everybody else
For you are your own best
It is about who you are
Not about who you were
Forget every scar
Forget all the fear
It is time to start over
It is time to stand tall
Learn to love yourself better
It is the greatest love of all
You are the shining star that shines for ever and brightens
from afar when sky gets darker
You are bright like the sun
You can burn or you can shine
You are your own horizon
Set or rise at your skyline

Love At First Sight

It is like a nectar
And we are the butterflies
Which flutter
From one flower
To another
In a garden of flowers
Indulging in the nectar's sweetness
Until there is no more
Until there is no reason to stay
Nothing worth waiting for
So we flutter away
To a new flower
And the cycle goes on for ever

Love at first sight
Can it be right?

RIJUL ALFRED

Rijul Z Alfred is an energetic focused high school student from Delhi, India. She's just 14 but speaks directly from the soul. Her poems have remarkable momentum and depth. She is also an A+ math student who has passion for singing as well.

Nature Lover

All my happiness is hidden on the gaze upon u
Time by time, the joy towards u is no more few
Raise ur words, Not ur voice
It's Rain that grow flowers not thunder's noise
Life is not about storm to pass
It's learning to dance in the rain's glass
Here I can listen to my inner voice
And realised! to success, I hve millions of choice
All things r beautiful for the person who caries happiness
within
Whoever loves and understand a garden will find
contentment in him
People have turned weird to me
But in nature, I learnt to flee
In nature, I got cut off from the world
And got so many things pearled
U r as beautiful as I wanted
And ur silence is as great as I nominated
Caught in her eyes

Unfailing Love

a invocation it prayed
Crying in bed it layed
Night with joint hands
Another but a wrong demand
So focusing , it asked
Promised to change the past
 a prayer to the God most high
impossible if he didn't reply
then it saw, it got more beautiful
than the prayer not replied
A graceful hand
Picked me up when I can't even stand
Unfortunately it realized
It was replied in a beautiful style
His most wierd lost child ever
Still he decided to love me forever

Broken Fantasy

Hate the changes got
Without any gun was shot
Alive with dead don't be shock
Cuz all this is what u hve brought
Gorgeous eye also sees same world
 You too once served
Wanna tell everything
But why is your voice a shrill?
Your anger express by hurting words
Mood was changed but remain words
Hurting the first moment
Stronger turn the second exponent
Was taught it's wrong
It will pain for long
Broke the fantasy
Before the starting of tragedy

Incomplete Puzzle

Am i making excuses to myself?
I still put ur things upheld
Hard enough to explain in words
Allowing songs to hurt me I heard
One with a purpose
Master of misery in a circus
Tell, this is not the reality
But its not even like artificiality
When came to know what all it was for
Already all of it was lost
Like a puzzle finding the last missing piece
Lost everything, even my peace
Hiding feelings by fake words
Sinking and sinking in this world
Finally got the last piece of the puzzle
Ohh! The puzzle is lost in the struggle

So Called Sixth Sense

Floating in a black hole
Who's top is closed
Crashing my world filled with feelings
Into smittherness and pieces
I have lots and lots on my plate
Feelings in a line like fail
Learn to say "I really haven't got hurt"
Do feelings have any concern?
The path I shared is rippled
The causeway of destiny is not little
Dependents too feel
After hurting will they heal?
Put your feet into the shoes of a sufferer
You'll run away from the shoes further
Feel the wrong you did is still spreading
The one you hurt is still shreding

JENISHA SHAH

Jenisha Shah is a girl from Mumbai, India. She is 23 and has graduated Bachelor of Commerce. She is a girl who started writing poems from the year 2017.Till now she has written more than 200 poems from which she will put down few of them. A girl who loves to experience different things in different fields and loves to spread practical and positive approach to the world through poems. Her other interests are dancing, styling and travelling.
Email id-jenisha518@gmail.com
Instagram id-a_way_to_express

Unborn Child

I want to go out,
Out of this world,
The world I am packed in,
For my mother it is precious more than gold.
Soon I will come out of my cage,
I promise I will make you proud dad, who earns wage,
I know you are feeling a kick,
It is just a sign that I am coming quick.
You will be waiting when will I come out,
When will I cry my first shout ,
You will be waiting to touch my soft small feet,
Which are clean and neat.
I am waiting to come in this world,
Where I have my mom and dad very old,
Who have crossed difficulties to make me mild,
I will make you'll happy and that's a promise from an
UNBORN CHILD.

Distinct People

You have a different vibe with every person,
Each and every person teaches you a different lesson,
Some people control your mind,
Others are totally mild.
With some people you feel tranquil to share,
Some people's aspect are very rare,
There are some people we look up to,
And some people who don't give up on you.
There can't be one person whom you can select,
Because every person has their own flair to reflect.

It's All About Time

It's not in your hand once it is gone,
It has changed from the moment when you were born,
You need to get up and do what you want,
Be in present, is what it grants.
It will fly and you will look back to it,
Just make sure it is lit,
Love life and live in present to the fullest,
You don't know your future, what it presents.
So make the most of the moment or else you will regret your crime,
It' all about how you are making the most of your TIME.

Love

It's so easy to go with the flow,
You will get right up, together when you are low,
Praying for them and seeing their smile is all you want,
Not getting to know where they are, will make you haunt.
Caring and understanding will come in, and you won't realize it,
Adjustment and changes will automatically transmit and fit,
It can be with your family, life partner or friends ,
Because being secured with each other is what you need till the end,
Once you get that vibe together you will grow you light,
Because LOVE is where together you will fight and won't ever leave their sight.

School Memories

Entering the school on our first day,
Who thought it will be a memory one day,
The feeling of having our new friends,
Celebrating it through colourful friendship bands.
Never thought we will ever move apart,
The memories which are still in our heart,
The craziness we did in the class,
Waited for the result , will it be first or second class.
We had so much fun in our trips,
Where clothes used to pop, once the bags were unzipped,
Worrying about the sports day, will we be able to do it,
Between four houses we all use to compete.
We all our growing and learning,
We never thought school memories were , what we are earning,
Where during march-past we burnt our calories,
Those were our SCHOOL MEMORIES.

CINDELLA BROWN

Cindella Brown is a full time student in small town, located in California. She is on her way to become a Registered Nurse. When she is not studying for school she have many hobbies that include creative writing, painting, and her love for makeup. She is extremely passionate and a bit eccentric to some but it is her heart of gold that leave an imprint on many lives.

Karmic

She took a journey waves roaring and stormy weathers, ancient knowledge was discovered, feelings were activated and developed and lessons were learned. Torn between spreading her wings and letting go or holding onto love and afraid of the unknown. She learned to loosen her grip on control and surrender. Many trials, errors, and redos. Now she must make the decision to choose herself. She has learned enough,
This time... she didn't wait for his text nor had the heavy feelings of a broken heart. Of course she was sad but also a tad bit relieved as she felt peace in her own solitude and now her inner voice sounded more assured than ever.

Dark Souls

Arizona sky and California sky
Two different individuals cross paths
Remember you mentioned "beyond two souls" that one night and we somehow ended up singing Frank ocean to Michael Jackson until you told me "goodnight".

Endless phone calls and conversations about rendezvous and future plannings. Spontaneous vacations from Arizona to California.

Heat to heat
Skin to skin
The touch of your lips
Sweet ecstasy and bliss

Remember that one fall night
We were in the hotel room loaded off of fun pills that made us giggle and our tears spill on to one another. Your guard fell and my heart opened that night.

A deep bond was formed between two opposites no matter how different
Somehow destiny brought us together on this path

We Were both weary of love but gave it a shot just to see how long it would last, you gave me a feeling of love I did not know existed
I was so blindly in love with you at the beginning...before the mask fell off
I swore I had it all figured out, that you will be my last
That is before the ego and lies showed their faces and I just could not play pretend
Somehow
The darkness found its hold on our love.
How could something so beautiful end so tragic and just like magic I wanted to escape what reality was showing me
Next thing I know I'm being lead away from
You, my sweet love.

Separation

I miss the old you
Where did you run to
It's not fair for you to leave and not care
I miss the old you
Where have you gone too
Please come back home soon
Because I can't live without you.
You been so different
I can't get though to you
This just isn't like you
Where did you go to
Please come back home soon
I can't do this thing called life without you
Oh baby I miss you I can't forget you
All that we been though it's not worth disappearing on
Oh where did you go too baby please come back soon

I'm crying my eyes out
Waiting out this drought
Missing you led to sprouts of depression repressed emotions,
past life regression
Oh lord just send me a message of progression.
I'm sitting here by the window pane of hallow darkness
calling out your name
The silence of isolation left me astray.
Will things ever be the same
change sinks it's teeth into you and swallows you whole, and
spit you out into territory unknown.
This life is crazy man
Cycles of lessons just to get to where your destined.
Oh where did you go to I can't live without you please come
back home soon.

Blood Galore

Blood filled the tub that night Also with lust and lies and maybe love. Blood filled the tub My eyes blurry from the overflowing blood shooting from between my legs Not only was blood leaving my body but so was my love for you. Creation is nothing to play with Life fell out of me Memories of our first meeting replayed We weren't supposed to come this far Everything moved so hastily with us We did not know how to slow down You put your seed into me But couldn't see into me Couldn't see the endless possibilities Of what the future will hold So of course you fold And leave me all alone With a stone in my heart And scars and memories of our deceased baby, You left me here on my own to digest this spiderweb of a mess you weaved so thick around me I still have strings attached, that keep pulling me back to you I wish they all would collapse Like buildings from an earthquake Shake and shake and shake Until Every web of lie or doubt And hesitation falls from my pitiful frame Until every fragment of you fall and break You are a snake that slithered its way into my heart , tangled yourself around it and squeezed just to see if It would bleed. Now all I can do is weep Take me away from the pain Take me away from the deceit Take me away from Arizona This place is just not for me.

The Final Farewell

He cupped my face with his brown warm hands my cheeks felt smothered with pressure   My endless tears dropped onto his knuckles His slightly parted eyes pierced my tear filled ones....we knew it was goodbye, the space around us filled with magnetic tension but the air smelt like change, crisp and fresh. Both afraid of the unknown of life's treasures, both letting go of one another and learning to go with the flow, and to test one's ambition without comfort...sadness filled this young couple but also bravery, two souls separated but both gained their individuality, thankful forever thankful they both agreed on that at least.

LINDIWE SAKALA

Lindiwe Sakala is a writer, a basketball player and a student at Eden University. She's 18, and loves to write poems. Her poems are not all about herself but change.

Email: lindysakala2@gmail.com
Instagram: lindiwe_sakala
Writco: lindy_Tolile

My God

God!
Who is he?

People act like they dont know who he is
But guess what
You see God everyday you just don't recognize him

People think when there are no miracles
There is no God
And that he doesn't exist

Take a look around
You yourself are proof that he exists
If it wasn't for your existance you would have had doubt
Your life is a miracle
And you should be greatfull
Wise up
And be an example

Preparation and Rapture

By failing to prepare . You are preparing to fail. Don't say I will do it tomorrow. How long will you keep on saying that... Prepare and your day will come. The best preparation for tomorrow is today. Leave your life like Christ is coming this afternoon . How would you want him to find you. Imagine Jesus coming and finding you doing the worldly things. When all you said was I will start tomorrow . You know what, let's start now . Let's win souls . Let's give. Let's preach the word. Your bible is the light, the word of God has everything. When you begin to discover who you are there is no one who can do anything to you. All things are ready if our mind be so I know it's crazy to believe in silly things, But you look so very pure when you suffer from your addictions…

Dear brothers and Sister , Rapture is real. The coming of our Lord Jesus Christ is real. Do not be deceived by non believers . Utilize your Bibles . The word of God has everything . Romantic love is deeper than reality; it is more complex, intricate, fragile, and ethereal than reality. Reality does not inspire the exhilaration and ecstasy of love. Imaginative persons whom believe in love experience the exhalation and poetic frenzy of rapture.The greatest force in this world is love, you can't give too much, you can't take to much and you can't remain with. NothingThere is no fox stronger than love... Even the terrorist have someone so dear to them.

Happiness, peace and love

Very little is needed to make a happy life. Friends, Family or even Food. It is all within yourself. A happy life cannot be without a measure of darkness. The word Happy would lose its meaning if it was not balanced by the word Sadness. Happiness is when what you think,
What you do. And what you say is in harmony. Some cause happiness wherever they go. While some seek happiness wherever they go. A person lacking happiness is like an empty shell. It has no value yet people still get attracted to it. A peaceful mind is a peaceful heart. You will never find peace of mind until you listen to your heart . Love is not something you feel, it's something you do. Love and peace of mind protects us and teaches us to overcome the problem that life has at hand. We live in a life of victory. We see different things and overcome different things. You chose to wear a smile or not. It doesn't matter, what matters is what you do within yourself.
I find happiness in living
I live in peace
And I find peace in love

Love

I wish I could explain your eyes How your smile gives me joy The sound of your voice makes my heart skip a bit Being around you makes me feel complete   Days spent together are the only memories I have of you You are my good days My once in a lifetime   I love waking up knowing you are mine   The only prettiest thing I remember capturing with my eyes wide open is your smile I miss my unique Babe I thought this distance would bring division But no Its the time to get things right To correct errors And get to understand each other   I feel for the negatives I did I'm glad I figured them out   A relationship is not always perfect But I feel the perfection is perfectly perfect

Rape

What wrong did I do Am I so unlucky Is this my fate Most of my friends are rape free But why me It hurts me, every time I recall the moment Some memories will forever remain fresh . I blame myself I blame the whole world Is everyone like that Is every adult like that I'm so afraid The world is full of dangerous people How can someone be so cruel No mercy,no pity A little child passes and all you think of is yourself Thoughts do matter Not one sided But both sided What will happen if I rape this kid What will we both benefit from As adults it's our duty to take care of little kids And not them fearing us Let's show love everywhere Little kids lives matter Say no to rape.

MANQOBA MTHETHWA

Manqoba Mthethwa is a 24 year old Poet from South Africa. He is a medical student who believes words have the power of healing. Diagnose with bipolar disorder Manqoba uses poetry to tell his story and give hope to others dealing with mental illness. With a flair for the dramatic he promises his words will make you feel his pain so that hopefull he'll know he is not alone.

Cursed

Cursed with unfortunate mishaps
That plague me with the mind of a cynic
I have never had a drink
But i would like to be hungover
And forget everyday that i have lived.
Wipe away all the agony i call memories
Maybe slip into a coma
Until i wake up in the future
Where they have found a cure fro a broken heart.

Different

I was told there's a beauty in the different
But i was never prepared for being treated like a freak
In a world run by neurotypicals you will regret being unique.
Every qwerk of yours ridiculed until you learn to hide your beautiful.
The world frowns upon abnormal like it's a defect to be original.
Time and again i have to remind myself I matter even though I'm unpopular.
They may try to box me but they can never cage my imagination.

Looking Forward To Death

If our lives are a gift
they why do you take them back?
If we were made in your resemblance
Why don't you share our flaws?
Why does a life so finite
get to determine our eternity?
I believe these questions matter
so I'm looking forward to death just to hear your answer.

Rainbows

I want to exist within these feelings
That overtake me
Be transported to a high
Of melancholy
Where rainbows are colourless
And rainfal drops in silence
From the clouds of my sadness.

My Companion

Most people don't have someone to come back home to.
I used to be the same before I met you.
I spent years unaware of what you can do.
Now you are shoulder that's sticks closer than a friend.
A worthy companion to whom I can depend.
When tears threaten to overtaking me, I turn to you instead.
I start to undo the damage with a pen in my hand.
You're the journal I united with in holy matrimony.
You right besides me no matter how vexing the journey.
Even if life were to destroy me I know you'll tell my story.

RICHARD CHARLES GWYN

He loved reading and writing since he was young. He wrote his first poem in grade 10. He has been writing for over 30 years now.

Lost

Before I met you I was lost
Like a sailboat drifting
In the middle of the ocean
I couldn't find myself
Alone for a very long time
Since meeting you
The shore was in my sights
Reborn and revived
I swam to land
I left the boat behind
And everything in my past
Now the future is bright
I only want to look forward
And I never want to look back

Vanish

Together we can disappear Never again to reappear The two
of us with no fear Forever calling each other dear United we
could just vanish Go somewhere and learn Spanish Or far
away and forget English Visit someplace and eat a Danish Go
and forget all of our troubles Erase all of our fails and fumbles
Delete the cause of our tumbles With you all my problems
crumble

You Are Amazing

You are beautiful in mind body and soul
You are the envy of any other
You give life to a room when you enter
You make everything more valuable
You bring light into anything dark
You give hope to anyone in despair
You could turn water into wine
You could turn coal into diamond
You make everyone so much happier
You turn frowns completely around
You are simply astonishing and rare
You are ..plainly stated.. are just so unique

Bullies

It's always something they say So very rude and inconsiderate Speaking like we are beneath them Treating us like imbeciles Mocking they way we speak Teasing us the way we dress Physically hurting us Punched and kicked Mentally scarring us Words that cut deep Emotionally harming us Using our feelings against us Soon one day the tables will turn The hunter will become the prey Karma arrives and it will cease They will not get away

Grand Parents

They begin when you're a baby
Spoiling you with toys
And stuffed animals
Always willing to babysit
To spend time with their grandkids
When you start to walk
They want to take you places
The park or the beach
If the parents allowed it
They would take you on trips
To a different country
They are very wise
Beyond their years
They know more than they let on
They let you get away with stuff
Which is why you always should love them

SOHITA SAPKOTTA

Sohita Sapkotta is 24 year teacher from Alipurduar, West Bengal. A jovial gigglemug by heart,logolepsic, melophile and lover of sketches. Art for her is a way of life and poetry is like those little inns where she stops to rejuvenate herself in this long journey. Metaphors always makes her day. She holds a perception that nothing changes in life, its we who grow .

Petrichor

It followed the scorching heat, the blistering summer.
Yelling the chiliad hearts and it's beat ;
The wait was full of dreams,
of encapsulating the aroma within.
The splashing raindrops and the gentle whiff,
wetpained the Orb with words it couldn't speak.
The thirst intemperate was not quenched,
 the turf moaned the sky ;
Nature : the kind, listened the whispers ,
bidding the Sun goodbye.
Is it real or a semblance !
Who could clear it in a glance ?
But the savour strayed today, somewhere in the Lands.
Oh dear'ly Petrichor! The Queen of Olfacs.
Are you in Souls or lost in the Sins ?
I search you every Rains ,
Where are you in ?

The Lone Shingle

I was the foreshore sand and
You were the lashing whitecap ;
You've touched me a thousand times,
But there was always a gap.
Well, You never stopped your part
Though I never spoke a word.
Maybe you wished a day comes
When I ll rock your world.
Touching me was fair,
or it wasn't or what is it !
My silence left you in a despair.
But Hey! Why do You still drench me ?
by the every iota.
Are You in the urge that I dunk you up.
Remember, You are big blue ocean,
I m a mere speck of sand ;
We can never walk together
hand in hand.

Tales of Innocence

Its been a decade since I stepped this place , though it's only fifty footsteps away my home- Grandpa's Farm - " My Happy Little Home"
I remember my toddler days when I caught my Hajuba's finger and walked down these green fields. He made us pick some herbs and berries, also some corn in spring. I also remember how carefully I walked over those mud pavements as I was messy with clayey roads. Those fake pretending child labour and those mid break brunches and the poppins candy which Hajuba bought for us.
Everything was so soothing. Life was fun, easy and lovely.
Well,The grass here is still green but the greenery somewhere faded inside me.
I no more go to find those herbs and berries now, as there's no one to give me a candy in return for the work I do.
All that's left here is only silenced breeze which tells no tales.

I miss you Hajuba

San Nani

Lacuna

A boulevard never walked , a flower never plucked,
A rainbow never touched, was there a heart always judged.
Her eyes had the death like a trench in a sea,
A Thaumaturgy anyone could see.
She was an incessant flow of parole in an epic,
The fathom of which had no prosaic.
Her twilight's croon left thousands soul soothing,
But somewhere in her solitude,
She lived with a Lacuna within.
Holding the sultry Sahara within,
Her journey towards the frigid frost began.
She walked spreading the colours of mirth and gay,
On the Eden's buds, branches and hay.
From hearts to hands, She could join everything,
But when on joining self, She still has a Lacuna within..
A Lacuna Within…

" APRICITY "

There is something disparately beautiful
about the Sun gingerly going South.
It is still a ball of bold and bright,
 but doesn't burns me anymore.
I open my casement every single morn
to see a patio of Granny's unseasonal corn.
Always are they fluttering and glistening,
singing a song which no one is listening.
Oh well, the Sun ! I gaze it more than others
Until tears roll down my cheeks.
Sometimes I stare, sometimes I snub
Sometimes it's just a morning Peek
Though called static, I never see it the same
There is something differently beautiful,
everyday in its flame.

NISHA SAINI

निशा सैनी एक कवयित्री और अध्यापिका है उनको लिखना बेहद पसंद है वह मानती है कि हमारे विचार ही समाज की परिस्थितियों को बदलने में सक्षम होते हैं   वह अपनी कविताओं के माध्यम से लोगों को जागरूक करना चाहती हैं वह मानती हैं कि कविताएं हमारे जीवन का सारांश होती है |

(1)

जो राहत दे दिल को
वो अल्फाज कहां से लाऊं
सच कहूं दिल कहीं लगता नहीं
तुमसे दिल लगाने के बाद

कुछ उलझे कुछ सुलझे
रिश्तो की कहानी रह गई
साहिल पर बैठकर देखा जब
मौजों की बस रवानी रह गई

आता है जब यादों का सावन
तो ये आंखें भीग जाती हैं
वक़्त के इन गलियारों से
तेरा चेहरा ढूढँ लाती हें

(2)

सरल नहीं खुद को पहचानना
सहज नहीं जीवन के यथार्थ को जानना
जीवन का सत्य जन्म और मरण का स्मरण जीवन के अवरोधों का
समतल अवतरण

अंकुर फूटता हो जैसे भूतल में
दूर पर्वत में नील बरसते हो झर झर में
किरण दूर भोर उजारे खेल के धूप सोना बरसा वे भेद कटावे प्रेम
कारोबार के दयार का

भीतर क्रोध का उज्जवल उद्गगम
धूल है ,धुंध है शोर ही शोर है
चंद्र किरण को छोड़कर चकोर घनघोर है
ना सरोवर, ना पपीहरा ठंडी छांव सिरमोल है

(3)

मुश्किलें आती रहेंगी
ना डर इन आंधियों से
यह झोका है हवा का
हौसलों की जिद का
खुद से लड़
आराम ना कर
जीवन का पथ है मुश्किल
इसे आसान ना कर
डर कर सिमटना कैसा
यू राहों से फिर भटकना कैसा
सरल ,सहज सतत संघर्ष है
गिर कर उठना ही जिंदगी का समर्पण है
बिखर जाए हार कर तो
फिर संभलना होगा
यह जिंदगी है जनाब
आसमा से अपना बादल खुद ही छांटना होगा
दर्द की दीवार
कितनी भी लंबी हो
समुद्र की गहराई को सीप के मोतियों से नापना होगा

(4)

मुझे किसी बंधन में मत बांधो के मुझे बंधना नहीं आता उड़ता है दिल आसमां में मेरा की जमी पे चलना मुझे नहीं आता ना तम्मनाओं की बरखा है ना ख्वाहिशों का पिटारा है। चलता चला में जिस राह पर ना जमी थी मेरी ना आसमां था मेरा सागर की लहरों सा उफनता मन इन्द्रधनुष के रंगों सा बिखरता मन सप्तरंगी आकाश का उज्ज्वल मन सपनों में तराशा उफनता सा स्वपन

(5)

खुद से खुद का वादा है। कभी दर्द कम,, तो कभी ज्यादा है।। ना गिरे.... आँखों से आंसू अभी। वक़्त का थोड़ा तकाज़ा है।। तू पास नहीं.. अब मेरे। फिर भी तेरा अहसास है।। तुझसे अभी तक दूर ना हो पाए। ये कैसी" भूख " "प्यास है।। उदासी के तकिए पर। दर्द की फुहार है।। तू कब पास आये मेरे। यही दिल की गुहार है।। ना जीते है.... ना मरते है। बस तेरी यादों के झोकों मे सोया करते है।।

TEJASVI MANOT

Hi Readers,

I Tejasvi Manot (Blagueur) - writer, artist and inspirational lover. I myself is a Fashion Designer by Profession.I 'm also a writer by my hobby.

I belive words are Such a creation that are mean't to play with them.

Basically I put love into my words and affection in the soul of the scentences.

Long Live The Lover's

Who are lovers?
Lovers are those who without thinking of others follows the relationship of love,
Lovers are those who takes part in each others good and bad times,
Lovers are those who has just one voice silence,
Lovers are those who worship love not treat it as a game.
Lovers are those who finds worth in every relationship,
Lovers are those who is democratic not dominant to each other,
Long Live The Lover's…………

Nature

You are so generous
You give us beauty,which we are greatful of,
You give us duty,which we are thankful of,
You give us peace,which we are graceful of,
You give us care,which we are boastful of,
You give us affection,which we are fruitful of,
You give teach us unity,which we are dutiful of
You teach us how to respect others,which we are delightful of,
Thanks for being so helpful to us..

Short Conversation With Dark...

Once I asked dark,That why am i here in darkness ?

Reply of dark...
You are here for peace of success.

I asked how?
He replied- coz darkness just don't means the black side of your life,it also can help you to see the brightest part of life which can lead you to success.

So Dark say's-Don't de affraid of me, I will make your life nice and brighter.

Toh Acha Hai

Zuban ki iss teer se kisiko ghayal na karo toh acha hai,
Apni soch se kisi ko nicha na dikhao toh acha hai,
Apne waqt se sabhi nahi tohkisi pal ko ji bhar ke ji lo toh acha hai,
Sath na ho par phir bhi dusro ko yeh ehsas dila pao toh acha hai,
Sishe main dekh kar khud ki buraiyon ko pahchano toh acha hai,
Kuki buri soch hoti hai insan nahi,
Kuki bure karam hote hai waqt nahi,
Kuki bure shaks hote hai sakshiyat nahi,
Toh apne buraiyon ko acha karo toh acha hai..

Naa jane

Naa jane kitno ki aayat ho tum,
Naa jane kitno ki khwahish ho tum,
Naa jane kitno ki riwayat ho tum,
Tumhari ruhaniyat na jane kitno ko zehenaseeb karar kar deti
hai,
Naa jane tum kitno ko fanna kar deti hai,
Naa jane kitno ki rooh ko tum innayat karar deti ho,
Kya khub tumko banaya khuda ne,
Ki har khubsurat chiz ko sharminda karti ho...

SONIA-ROSE LYLE

While Sonia-Rose was completing her undergraduate studies at the University of Valley Forge, she shared spoken word poetry at youth events with a student-led ministry called: The Art Of. After she graduated in 2018, she published more poetry content on Instagram and Writco (global community mobile app for poets and writers). Sonia-Rose lives in the Uptown neighborhood of Chicago, Illinois, where she lives in an intentional community and serves on the production team at VIVE Church Chicago.

Remove Vanity

Remove vanity in us, Almighty God
Every day, vanity and humility are fighting at odds
Our flesh wants excessive attention from the world
On the other hand, excessive pride has led our inner beings to be intensely curled
Vanity of riches leads us to enjoy wealth and possessions with grievous evil
Everything done under the sun becomes vanity when we live under the power of the devil
Vanity fills our souls when we live outside of faith in the resurrected Christ
After death, everything we did apart from you will reap havoc as the Antichrist
Nothing will be done in vain when we turn away from darkness and trust you
All things work together for good those who are called according to your purpose and love you
Take away vanity and help us walk in humility
You said those who humble themselves will be exalted for your glory
Thank you for removing vanity in usYour name will get excessive attention in the midst of this ruckus

Remove Inner Confusion

Vicious cycles of confusion have led people to identify with a different gender

Each day with inner confusion gives people a lack of peace and false liberty

If only they knew the sacrificial death and resurrection of Jesus Christ, who is the world's only Savior

No one but Jesus was willing to give up everything to give confused people clarity

Remind people of the price Jesus paid for them to be with Him for eternity

Embrace them with your gentleness and love that they may be drawn to repentance

Restore inner clarity in their minds and fill them with your peace that strips off anxiety

Confusion is dead on the cross of Calvary that people become alive in your presence

O Spirit of God, replace confusion with clarity that they will embrace your redemptive work

Nothing is impossible for you because you are the One who preserves their confident clarity in Christ as a bottle cork

Upper Room Tribe

Unshakable by persistent prayers
Preparation begins for the big wedding of the bride of Christ and Christ the groom
Prayer and fasting begins after they walk up the stairs
Eventually, they arrive at the upper room
Rooftop shakes at the Spirit-filled prayers and cries of people
Rumors spread around that they were drunk though it was only morning
Others criticize until a man named Peter clarifies what happened to the people
On this day, the Holy Spirit pours out His presence in the upper room tribe while the day is dawning
Men and women receive His outpouring and declare God's word they have heard
Times of prayer and study of His word in the upper room fill people with joy overflowing
Rest comes to His beloved as they pray persistently with faith after He fulfills His word
In the midst of the outpouring, the upper room tribe is growing and expanding
Be in the upper room with the Holy Spirit
Every moment spent in His presence leads people beyond the mountaintop's summit

Distant Secret Place

Drawn away from the crowds. Idols and distractions removed. Stillness took place of the demonic thoughts that were loud. Total undivided attention to the Holy Spirit unmoved. A moment turns into a lifetime in the secret place. Nothing is better than spending time with the One who paid the penalty of our sins. The hours we spend in the secret place with the Holy Spirit will draw others to seek His face. Strife ceases as we walk away from chaos and walk towards His calm inn. Every piece of pain within us is exposed before His presence. Shalom flows within us when we rest in His peace. Restoration takes place when His blood covers our brokenness. Every rhythm of rest flows after our heads are uncovered from the fleece. Countless days in the secret place reveal our dedication to know Him personally. Each visit in the secret place is countless conversations with the Holy Spirit intimately.

Elevate The Everyday

Every day is an opportunity to encounter the living God. Language that speaks life will uplift the hopeless as a rod. As we call on the name of Jesus Christ, His Spirit will elevate us through our humility. The same Spirit that raised Jesus from the dead will give us true liberty. Each day has its own plot twists as the stories of Heinrich von Kleist. Tried by fire and made like Christ. He will raise us in glory after our bodies are temporarily buried in brokenness. Exhortation with the word of God will lift up souls from the weight of heaviness. Elevation of the everyday occurs when we invite the Holy Spirit into the everyday and witness His mighty work every day. Vibrancy elevates the every day with the miracles, salvations and mobilized people who reach out to others who are led astray.

COLLINS TAKUDZWA BIRIMHIRI

He draws inspiration from hate and criticism, He touches on various themes and brings motivation and hope to the uninspired, He enjoys reading, travelling and socializing

Unraveled Unruffled

Clarion noises escalating behind the shade
Trying to be brave in the midst of a purge
My heart is under a siege, surgent rage
I need urgent attention like a surgical patient
Patent rights distorted, my record obliterated
Underated by hypocrites without a Bipont
Past, present or future. I'm resilient
Take me away to safety, away from all the pain
I encounter without gain, let me flourish like a grain
Of mustard. This tiny drop of ink will make them think
Sickly thoughts diluted into a bottle of unhealthy living
Vices bring out the best of me more than eating healthy
Serenely mixing serendipity and insanity
Vanity of all vanities, I lost myself when I lost her smile
Time heals the wounds, mine get worse everyday
Her departure from my heart haunts me whenever she passes
by, She should have passed away maybe her memory would
have vanished
Her presence is like a rough hold but still I remain unruffled.

COMPETENT

Come close, don't shy away from the pain.
Keep your friends close and your enemies even closer.
Kiss me aggressively even though my breath is disgusting
This Gas sting badly like a provoked Bee
Sea or ocean view, late night cruise
Bruised, abused and viciously used.
Lady please! Stand up taller than the tower
Power is not given so take it and run with it for your emancipation.
Stagnation is worse than constipation because it stinks.
Women are the bearings of every wagon.
Lately their silence has been more deafening
The than the ruff rattling noises of these cowardly Man at pubs,
Beating women black and blue till their natural posture is in hue
Sue inconsiderate beings before they dig your grave.

FAIRYTALE LOVE

The Apple doesn't fall far from the tree, well
She fell and landed straight in my eye
Head over heels, She is my shelter.
Dealt with a hand of outrageous odds,
God's must be crazy to turn lovers against each other.
Love is lovely and in love is taciturnity.
Insanity of humanity is derived from hate.
Hurt my temple, break my heart.
Let me be distant from your contagious scent
Bent all the rules to be with the love of my life
So much for sacrifices, she did the same.
This is no fairy tale, I don't have a godmother.
True love still exists
My partner and I are a testimony.
Check the details of the ceremony.
This is a Holy Matrimon

Dance

Jump up and down
Don't be rigid
Timid and stupid
Rapid movement
Grooving in the moment
Remember my sweet ornament?
Now its a tournament
Experiment the supplement
Sacrament like a new testament
Adamant not a sediment
Denounce resentment...

Tragic Reality

My heart shuttered, cracked and stopped as they threw the last shovel .That was it, the end of the world, the end of my sanity. Agility lost and adrenaline sucked out expeditiously
Tenaciously we lived, but the hands of time refused to turn back.Take me away too, so I can be connected once
With the one that introduced me to this place filled with strange beings and things
Wings needed urgently so I can fly away and meet my maker. She contained me till the third trimester, Esther because of her Gesture
Posture, filled with the ability to detect an imposter. Yet they say she is in a better place as if anyone has visited there and came back
Back pack filled with all her favourite things as I prepare to journey
Towards oblivion, they probably won't remember me even with a medallion
"A thousand years is like a day and a day is like a thousand years" How much time do we get to live?
Do you believe in a better place when one dies?
Do you believe in live after death?
Answer me and make me happy.

VIZIICHU KAJIRI

Viziichu Kajiri is a student from Nagaland, India. Writing had always brought peace of mind and confident to her, so she wishes to share her writings to others and be a bit of their happiness.

Rookies

Not the best, but we are a total of six.
Outset from diverse vicinity.
Smashing group to some,
While unendurable to some.
Our presence known by our thunderous laughter,
Silent is something out of our dictionary.
Love and war always a tie,
Tears, we wipped off silently,
Joy, we declare aloud
We gossip faster than 4G,
At times, we're wild like the juvenile gangster,
But love, we do unconditionally.

Dissemble

Every sunrise, an addition to my phoney,
None to blame for my downfall.
Restrictions I give myself second,
Eyes, I begged everyday not to cry,
Heart I plead everyday to stop loving.
Everyone pisses me off,
Everything breaks me,
Still, laugh from dusk till dawn,
Cause there are too many judging me,
Too many doubting my panoptic happiness.
Wished to the stars a million times,
That every sunset will cease my pain,
And I'll finally walk without a fake smile.

Prospect Heart

Friends I called once, now a stranger,
Love I said once, now my foe,
Blessings I considered once, now not worth keeping,
Lifetime, I believed, didn't last a year.
Time will change adversely with me,
No blessing nor misfortune is constant.
Extant suffering will cease,
Tears will no longer flow,
Sleepless night I'd spend will give me rest one day,
My wreck heart will heal steadily,
As, none has proven finite luck,
Nor eternal misfortune.

Invisible Scars

She walks in beauty,
With her head held high,
As if goddess of Halcyon,
No tears flow from her charming eyes,
Cheerful as if sorrow has never clashed her path,
Laughter and felicitous were all that was panoptic.
Her ravishing glow blinding the truth,
None knew her grief,
Not her tears behind her laughter,
Not her scars behind her gorgeous body,
Every morning waking up
To fight her own battle with reality,
Love as her foster,
And smile as her weapon,
Hiding her scar perfectly from the world.

Unspoken

I love thee earlily, though not my first get-go,
Incoherent about outset, yet idolize ineradicable,
My therapy in every catastrophe,
Though my being paltry to thee,
Yet still blissful with thy being.
I love thee, unfeigned,
Though cognizant of thy cognitive content,
Though there's a soul irreplaceable in thy heart,
Memories irreplaceable in thy mind,
Yet, I wanna believe I've a chance.
I love thee unruffled,
Though my anticipation, just a nix,
My hope, an access to my trauma,
My love, an entree to my grief,
Yet my frail baffled heart cueing me to stay tranquil.

J GEER

J Geer is a writer, a golfer, a chess player, a sibling, and a highschool student. They are almost 16 years old and wish to go to law school. J spends a lot of time with after school activities, siblings, and friends. They write because it helps them express their thoughts and emotions with the world and because they really enjoy writing

(1)

Take me away from this dangerous world today.
For my siblings young and old
are dying before their told
hideous slurs and that they're not enough.
Well, we have had enough!
Homophobes and racists are loud
as the try to tear you apart with sound,
yet we stand strong as we move along.
The struggle of death is weakening
especially without valid reasoning
or one last goodbye.
So, to my grandpa fly high.
Grandpa I miss you dearly
and to my unmet siblings dying yearly
you are missed and fought for
your names yelled so no one can ignore
that people took your lives away
when you wanted to stay.
However, if you wanna know what I say
about this world I'll tell you "take me away"
Today is a day
the world holds her breath and waits
For it all to change

(2)

I wish the world was pure
I wish the world was kind
I wish the night was young
I wish these demons would leave my mind
I wish the pain could be taken away
I wish some people saw another day

(3)

Take me away now
Screams the thought in my head
That will always stay

(4)

Today is a new day
I can feel in a new way
I can be happy
or feel sappy
I can dance around
or lay on the ground
but I can not forget you
I know that is true.

GEETA SHUKLA

Geeta shukla is a writer, artist and a student from Gandhinagar, gujrat. She is pursing her master's from national forensic science University and she is a first year student. She started writing at the age of 17. The motivation of writing comes from novels. Her journey as writer start with writting quotation for school and then after for college as well. She loves to express whatever she observes or thought and to make people sees things in a positive way through her writing.

Her Soul Need Some Peace

She was 14 when this incident happened. She never thought that this happen to her. Riya have soo many dreams in her eyes, but that one incident took away everything. It was the holy summer days. Everyone go to their grand parents' home for holidays. Riya was soo excited to see her nephew or nice. She is there at her brother's place. She have many dreams for baby boy or baby girl. She take care of here Bhabhi with enthusiasm.

 Finally, the day come. She is blessed with a niece.

Doctor: congratulation it is a baby girl.

Riya: thankyou doctor for such a big news.

Doctor: its my job child. But baby is very weak, and her body temperature is also high.

 Doctors put her in ventilator because he baby girl is not in good condition she is suffering from some disease. They refer her to Banaras for further treatment. Riya's father and her mother take the responsibility for baby girl as her Bhabhi is also weak, so she need the support of her husband. Riya was in fear to lose her niece. She fall in love with the cute little baby girl. They leave the hospital in middle night with the baby girl. Her brother stayed there with her Bhabhi and tell Riya to go to home because no one was there. He called her cousin brother to take Riya home and also tell him to be with her this night and protect her. Nihal was 21 year. He is her Mausi's child. he look very handsome. He have bright skin tone. His eyes are perfect dark in color.

Nihal: let us go.

Riya: coming bhai.

Nihal: have you had your dinner?

Riya: not yet

Nihal: then let us go to some restaurant first.

Riya: no, no its alright we have something to eat. Mom made roti sabji for me before leaving.

Riya was very close to her cousins, so she have no problem with that. Her cousin brother took her to home. No one was there in home. She make him sit in her bed and ask for water or something to eat. He denied this but still she offer him a glass of water and went in kitchen. After completing the work in kitchen, she go to her room and open her wardrobe for night suit. Her cousin brother have eye on her. After change, the cloth she again go to her room and sit in her bed and switch on the television. She talk with her cousin brother about the day and about her studies. He is also share about his lifestyle and about his girlfriend. He was in relationship with that girl from past three years. The way he is talking about her looks like he is in love with that girl. Riya was very happy listing to his dear cousin brother's story that he is in love. She took an interest to know more about that girl or about their love story. He is also taking interest to

narrate his love story. She hug him and congratulate him for getting the love he need. It is 12 o'clock of mid night. Moon is at its peak. They finally go to sleep. He ask her if she have no problem then he will sleep in her room with her. She have no problem with this after all he is her brother. She make him sleep in her room. And this is the mistake she made. When she was in dreams, he touch her hand and sense if she is awake. She in very tired that within 10 min she is fully in her dreams. When is does not respond to the touch, he went closer to her and touch her legs .She feel something unusual and open her eyes. When she saw her brother close to her, she was in shock and for a minute she does not respond. When she came in complete sense of mind then she ask why he is close to her. Her brother sense that she probably get what he is doing. He hold her tight and hug her. She feel uncomfortable and push him back, but he never stop he hold her very tight ad start kissing her. She was in shock. Whatever happening is a bad

dream for her. She never ever thought that her cousin will do this with her. He pull her towards him and touch her upper body. She try to get apart from him, but his strength was too much for her. He kept saying you are too beautiful let do this no one will ever know this. She is shouting on him to leave her, but he never let her go. His hand move towards her breast. She kick him at his balls so to escape from his grip. This work the pain from e kick make him loosen the grip and she finally escape from there. She open the door of her room but forgot to close it. He follow her the whole way for her house. She hide herself on the roof top. But he caught her and just to protect herself from her cousin she jump out from the building. Her neighbors found her lying on the floor. She have sense they take her to the nearest hospital. She have fracture in her leg and some cuts on her body and a major injury on her head. Her cousin brother reach there after that. When she saw him, she start panic .People around her make her calm but she is not listening to them. The boy understand why she panic, and he left the room. After everyone go to their respective home. He enter in her room. She stare at him with lots of anger in her eyes.

Nihal: how are you?

Riya: why you came here, just get out from here.

(her eyes became red by anger)

Nihal: I told you we can solve it, no one get to know about this, but you took this stupid step.

(with a sarcastically smile on his face)

Riya: are you mad, did you forget I am your sister?

Nihal: you are not my real sister.

Riya: so, what

Nihal: what is the problem in this, you are beautiful I am smart.

Riya: I will show you what we are , once my mom dad came.

Nihal: oho I got scared. (in a sarcastic way)

Riya: you have to scared.

Nihal: do you think they will listen you?

Riya: of course, they have to listen to me.
Nihal: don't you know they love me more than you?
Riya: I am their daughter.
Nihal: so, what? you are younger.
Riya: get out from this room. (in angry tone)
Nihal left the room. The things Nihal said make Riya think about that. Her family love Nihal as he lost his other in cancer. He is the responsibility of her mom dad. She think what if her mom dad deny listening. A fear took place in her. She also not wanted to make her parents sham on her. Tears comes from her eyes the pain in these tears are much more than any pain. Her brother do this with her this is unexpectable for her. In an hour she lost everything herself self-confidence, strength, spiritual values, mind. She goes in hibernation this incident put a very big impact on her life. She start making her friends stay away from her. I hate to develop in her mind for boys. She start depriving to be with make friends. A lots of things in her mind run but she never share these thing with anyone just to be away from shame. The pain of this in her heart make her die day by day. She want to take away the pain and the memory of the incident from her mind, heart and from her life.

Sri Lasya Jillella

Sri Lasya Jillella is a student pursuing BTech in Computer Science from Nandyal, Andhra Pradesh, India. She is a writer , an author, dancer and motivational speaker. She is a Bibliophile and she feels that books are the best way to escape this harsh reality. She is a devotee of Lord Shiva and into the concepts of universe and spirituality. She feels that writing is the best way to let any mental trauma out and she is a seeker and explores the knowledge from the world and within.

Earth,A Weird Place Indeed!!!

Earth,yes the planet on which we live, cherish and make . We take birth ,growup ,learn ,laugh,cry and may more and in between the lanes we forget how to LIVE!!!

This has always been this way with you,with me and in fact everyone residing here. The way I told residing makes more sense as we have come to live here for a period of time and we all have to leave this place. We know that we definitely do know that we have to leave this place one day yet when any temptations attract us we forget,when problems surround us we forget the very basic fact that we are living here for a short time.well....this has been the problem with a girl too of whom I am gonna narrate.

She was a very innocent,gentle,bubbly and gentle soul who have come here like everyone of us. Her name was Shrishti. Like the name she has her heart holds no limits and she is a giver.

It was the time of her childhood where everyone must be falling, crying, laughing and chuckling but the fate that was in her life didn't make the things to be that way. She had to face her own grandparents abandonment as she was a girl and the reality was they expected a heir ,a boy who can hold their wealth and prosperity. They didn't give her enough love. Then next she saw with her own tender eyes of her parents arguing and fighting,as the age was hers she didn't understand why it was. Whenever tears fell down her mother's cheeks unknowingly her heart ached. Whenever her grandparents didn't embrace her and didn't give her love and care her heart ached and with that she saw the stars of whom her mom weaves stories that they are watching over us and they will

lead us the right way. Her mom's words rang in her head and stared at the stars praying,

"TAKE ME AWAY,I don't want to be here!!!"

"TAKE ME AWAY, no one loves me here!!!"

"TAKE ME AWAY, My parents argue daily!!!"

"TAKE ME AWAY, My own grandparents never came to visit me!!!"

Tears rolled down and she lost herself staring at the stars. They glowed back to her and she thought that they were smiling at her assuring her that Everything's gonna be fine. She wiped the tears headed towards her bubbly cheeks.

Days went and nothing got better but she understood how to deal with that then as she was now a teenager. She got into new school and new atmosphere took over her. She was not so the typical nerdy one but she was calm and silent. She was an introvert. She waited for people to come to her and talk yet no one came to her. On seeing her fellow students going together she too wanted to be one of them and like them. Yet no one came to her. No one ever noticed her presence or absence.The fact was no one didn't give a damn about her. She was hurt. It broke her tender heart. And there came that phase of her life that she ever crushed on a guy. They guy was a school topper. She liked him, she was attracted to him and she loved him like never. Life is all different if it goes according to our will and wish it wouldn't be called life it had to break us and it had to make us. She decided to propose him and she did so finally but what she was returned with a rejection a very hard core rejection. This time her soul was shattered. She just couldn't share that with any let alone be her parents and mom. She did

the only thing that she can and she could too. Staring at the distant stars who were smiling at her she said with the silent sobs escaping her from her depths of the heart and soul.

"TAKE ME AWAY, I am not good enough!!!"

"TAKE ME AWAY, I am not loved by any !!!"

"TAKE ME AWAY, No one ever cared about me!!!"

"TAKE ME AWAY, I was badly rejected!!!"

"just TAKE ME AWAY,I just can't take any more pain!!!"

As she prayed for nothing changed as usual the only thing changed was time. She spent days crying for him and feeling bad about her that something lacked in her. Time is the best healer. We all know it and it did that magic. As the time went by she slowly was able to divert her thoughts from him but never forgot him. The one true love it was she just couldn't forget. Now it was the time for her college. There came struggles for money. Her mom's health worsened and they had to sell their house for her cure. No she had no hope left for higher studies too.She felt dejected,she felt rejected by Everything, by God,by nature, by stars,by people and almost everyone she felt worthless. She suffered a lot as her mom's treatment went on and she had to stay with her at hospital as there were no one whom she can rely on to and there were no relatives,well wishers and friends too. This time she silently stared at the stars. She had no prayer left ,no tears left, no heart left,no feelings left, no care left , moreover no LIFE left.

There comes a miracle in everyone's life. But all we need to do is recognise it and accept it. Life gives us every opportunity to improve oneself,to heal and to move on and it depends on oneself whether to accept it and move towards our improvement or stay there stagnate ourselves and our life blaming others, circumstances and people. Well... it's a choice to choose from. There came that miracle in her life too but unlike many of us she chose to take that not for herself but also for her parents and the people around suffering like her.

The financial support reached her and she joined the university. Life was like the other side now. It was on her side now. She got the best education, teachers and most importantly she got the best friends on her back. She had people around who cared and wanted her welfare. As the time flew by she was hired in a very reputed company with a well paid job. She moved on with her friends to the new world and she embraced the new journey. Her life took a tremendous turn. She had floods of money reaching her and her parents were proud of her and happy too. They became the happiest parents on the planet.

She had to move to a new city,and she was contented with her life. She never had to turn back from then nor did she had to stare at the stars out of misery. Love comes to you when you finally understood your worth. The fact it was and she met her significant other in the journey. Meeting him she felt that she found the missing piece of her life. He was her equal, in maturity, emotional stability, and Spiritually awakened like she was by the journey she had gone through. They both married with their elders consent. There was nothing which bothered her then. She has parents , a loving husband and an amazing life. She looked forward to know what life has got in store for her.But one day it happened the tragic of the story.

She met with an accident one night as she was going home from her night shift. Her husband was out of station and she decided to take a cab. But luck doesn't favour everyone

always. The mere fact it was and a truck hit her. She fell on the road in a span of a second blinking and hardly in consciousness. Red liquid spread all around her and her phone blinked with the id LOVE ,she could hardly see anything when her gaze fell on the phone. At that moment she didn't have anything in her mind,nor the blood, nor the pain she was going through,nor in the struggle she was.... recalling the beautiful moments of her life and the dreams of her life ahead she wanted to LIVE.....She wanted to live to cherish with her husband,she wanted to live for future,she wanted to live to share her memories with her children,she wanted to live to share her love and affection to her children she really wanted to LIVE.The stars stared down at her. She could see them. She forced a smile at them as she again found them smiling at her. She did the thing ever again.

"dont TAKE ME AWAY.... I have my responsibilities!!!"

"don't TAKE ME AWAY....My husband can't live without me!!!"

"don't TAKE ME AWAY.....I have a beautiful life ahead!!!"

"don't TAKE ME AWAY...I deserve to be loved!!!"

"don't TAKE ME AWAY...I have to be an inspiration to the world!!!"

"don't TAKE ME AWAY....I still have my responsibilities towards the people and world!!!"

"don't TAKE ME AWAY....this is not fair!!!"

"don't TAKE ME AWAY.....I wanted to LIVE!!!"

And darkness conquered her sight and she lost her consciousness. The next time when she opened her eyes she was on the hospital bed and the first thing she noticed was her MAN was beside her. Tears fell down but this time out of happiness and gratitude. She closed her eyes thanking the beautiful stars for having given her another chance to live and cherish. After recovering herself she did what she has promised them. She strived for the upliftment of the people who have gone through so much like her and she stood as a life support for all them. She stood as an inspiration ,as an example for all. She stood as a epitome of HUMANITY.

Finally at the end of the each day....she spent some time watching the stars, thanking them for everything that they have given her....the pain, the lessons,the problems, happiness, Prosperity and abundance. Well....if it was not for that pain and lessons....she would never be the way she was.And moreover she was HAPPY in her life.

Our life too has got so many things and the thing to be not forgotten is there is no one on this planet without problems and pain. Its all their maturity on how they are dealing it by masking them. Everyone can express their self pity but not everyone can give us the lessons by overcoming that pain. Life without problems is a fruit without taste. Problems are what break us and make us. Every problem has a solution and the solution is by being strong and fighting against it.Not give up. The life here is very empowering,we can learn everything here. And Life surprises you with something when you expect in the least and turning down at something when you have expected the most. This is the life here....thats why I say...Earth,a wierd yet BEAUTIFUL place indeed!!!

SANDY SALT

Sandy Salt was born in Sydney , and raised from 10 in South Australia, Is now 30 with 7 kids, writes to escape the pain, kicked out of school in yr10, rebellious , trauncer, black sheep, wanted to be an actress. Loves dance, drama, gymnastics tap, her family and friends.

I think it's time, I think it's time for my goodbye, I have felt pressure in my life I have always thought about suicide but it's different when u get deeper in disguise,
 that mask it weighs u down it takes over your soul it takes who you are, with no support anymore,
I ain't see shit to fight for, cos as sad as it is humans find their confidence in others, even if your like me ya typical
"don't give a fuck",
 " run ya mouth"
rebellious kid,
you still have a part of you even
the tiniest bit inside you
that makes you question you EVERYTIME
 someone don't like you,
like what's with me
 what is it about me
why did I hear that this person ain't judgmental,
 but I felt the most judged at that point,
the main ones that tear you down are
the ones you choose, the ones you can't and the ones you have spent most of your time with laughing and smiling their opinions matter the most,
 if they think your amazing, your on cloud 9
if they suddenly went from I love you
 your amazing
 how did I get you to wait a minute
 I got something to do, your feral
 I ain't even know why I'm with you ,
that shit changed overnight,
how that make you feel
 how that effect ur mentality
did it make your confidence rise
cos your a battler ur always down for the fight,
or did it make you weaker ,cos your tired of fighting
 you need some time off your feet, you need some reassurance,

you sick of proving what your worth,
like if people really cared instead of rarely
shouldn't I see what they all say about this shit called love
 is it not the only free thing on the planet, is it not the one thing
u can't buy it's the one thing you can't plan but at the same
time, is it not the best thing to let it go
and do what it do,
cos cupid shot me with an arrow
ur name babii it is engraved,
but when he shot mine at you, I'm almost certain
he nearly missed u only got grazed,
can barely see the scratch, your lucky I guess,
I'm wearing the worst of this,
 the worst of us, your leaving you can't take it,
all cos no one accepts you
 but what you don't get is this clichè right here,it ain't you it's
me,
 I am always gonna be the disappointment in my family
 I don't think they ever want me in a relationship, honestly,
 not unless it's with whom they choose
and I ain't the type, to do what I'm told,
I'm the type to literally do the opposite, i don't get this life
 I ain't understand a thing about this journey
 I know I been a difficult
and wasn't always the nicest person,
but I never once thought sacrifice would be my best option,
the best option for the kids, and him,
 I can't forget about the fiancee, the boyfriend, the best friend,
or is he the ex ,
well I ain't certain, today it's one thing the next it's another,
who knows anymore
 I ain't know shit about my life
it's only here to be run by others
I'm like a robot but I ain't gunna live for ever
 my energizers are running low, they are running out

I fear I'm on the last straw,
 im shaking right now cos I feel it in me
if only u knew the half of it
u might even start to try to understand but we both know
u couldnt, actually, possibly, really fully comprehend
 or completely,
understand me and the reasons behind why I am, who I am,
I ain't no saint no!
 I never preached to be something I ain't,
I am a soldier, I own who I am,
 my rep is all I have ever had,
since my dreams where ripped out from under my feet at age
10 cos what I wanted ain't matter to anybody
 I was only there doing what others wanted me to do,
and I'm still here doing the same shit too,
but I have lost everyone, and even worse I've lost all I am,
 i ain't got a fuckiin clue who that bitch is in the mirror,
I hear it's my reflection,
but I ain't ever met her during the fuckiin process,
I don't know what to do, I think it's my time, I feel it and
when god calls you home, U gotta go now it's my turn
 that's my name that's being called, that's my phone call home..

ARIEL PAUL

Ariel Paul is a woman who's Heaven Sent. A woman who wishes to make growth and love a movement. One who wishes to embrace the difference in the life we live in and make the best of it. Her difference lies in the way she unravels everything with the use of her words and her heart. While she discovers herself, it will truly inspire you to discovers parts of you too.

Mood

What do you call that feeling
Where I'm standing and there's nothing
Standing between me and the thoughts
I gotta turn into reality?

Gathering every inch of self to achieve
What they didn't believe.
This that thing that got me feeling,
You know...
Different.

Thinking that I'm powerful,
But that power anit all me.
As much eyes witness
An epitome of what a woman should be,
I'm humbled and cloth with grace
That the man above dripped me in.
That feeling is God sent
I'm Heaven Sent.
No words,
No image,
Nor, external validation
Could help express this feeling.
I just hope in due time you feel it too.

Flairs and Glairs, a platform by a student for the students. We are esteemed youth struggling to carve out our path for our future and we follow a basic mindset Since everyone is not born with all-round skills. Joining hands with people who are born to execute it with perfection is the best way to evolve. Self-Evolution is the need of the hour but, evolving as a community is what we strive for. The initiative as kickstarted by, Founder- Mr. Shubham Shah with the motive to utilize the skillset and talent of writing has now a team of 10+ people who are actively participating into newer forms of learning and discovering talents among youngsters. We Provide platform and services like Publishing opportunities, Open mics, Workshops, Hands-on training. Operating with Brand Name of Flairs and Glairs (Publication House), we offer the chance of elevating a passionate writer to an esteemed author With Brand name Teekhe Zasbaaat. We bring to you an opportunity to get accustomed with the Public Speaking and Presenting of Thoughts along with regular challenges to brush up your inking spirit. The newest initiative to extend our services we introduced in a new writing Platform- The Glittering Fables and Ink Over Tears.

We Choose to Fly Like A Falcon than to be

a Leg Pulling Crab.

To Know More: Infoline – 7781900870
Mail Us At-
flairsandglairs@gmail.com / info@flairsandglairs.in
Or Visit is at
www.flairsandglairs.com / www.flairsandglairs.in
Social Handles- @flairsandglairs @teekhezasbaaat